Translated Language Learning

Alice's Adventures in Wonderland

爱丽丝梦游仙境

Lewis Carroll

刘易斯·卡罗尔

English / 普通话

Down the Rabbit Hole
兔子洞

Alice was beginning to get very tired
爱丽丝开始变得非常疲倦
she was sitting by her sister on the grass bank
她和姐姐一起坐在草地上
but she had nothing to do
但她无事可做
her sister was reading a book
她的姐姐正在看书
once or twice Alice peeped into the book
爱丽丝有一两次偷看了这本书
but the book had no pictures or conversations in it
但这本书里没有图片或对话
"what use is a book without pictures?," thought Alice
　“没有图片的书有什么用呢？”

"why would a book have no conversations?"
“为什么一本书没有对话？”
but she had other things to consider
但她还有其他事情要考虑
"making a chain of daisies would be a pleasure"
“制作一串雏菊将是一种乐趣”
"but is it worth the effort of getting up and picking the daisies??"
“但是，值得起床摘雏菊吗？？”
this was not so easy to think about
这可不是那么容易想的
because the day was making her feel sleepy and stupid
因为那一天让她感到困倦和愚蠢
but suddenly her thoughts were interrupted
但突然间，她的思绪被打断了
a White Rabbit with pink eyes ran close by her
一只粉红色眼睛的白兔在她身边跑来跑去

There was nothing overly remarkable about the rabbit
这只兔子没有什么特别了不起的
and Alice did not think the rabbit remarkable either
爱丽丝也不觉得这只兔子很了不起
nor did it surprise her when the Rabbit spoke
兔子说话时，她也没有感到惊讶
"Oh dear! I shall be too late!" he said to himself
　"噢，天哪！我来不及了！
but then the Rabbit did something that rabbits didn't do
但随后兔子做了兔子没有做的事情
the Rabbit took a watch out of its waistcoat-pocket
兔子从背心口袋里掏出一块手表
he looked at the time and then hurried on
他看了看时间，然后匆匆忙忙地继续说
Alice got to her feet, in amazement
爱丽丝惊奇地站了起来
she had never seen a rabbit with a waistcoat before!
她以前从来没有见过穿背心的兔子！
nor had she ever seen a rabbit with a watch!
她也从来没有见过带手表的兔子！
Alice was burning with a new curiosity
爱丽丝又燃起了新的好奇心
and she ran across the field after the Rabbit
她追着兔子跑过田野
she was just in time to see the rabbit disappear
她正好看到兔子消失了
the rabbit hopped down into a large rabbit-hole
兔子跳进了一个大兔子洞
In another moment, down went Alice after the rabbit!
又过了一会儿，爱丽丝追着兔子倒下了！
The rabbit-hole went straight on like a tunnel
兔子洞像隧道一样笔直地向前
and the tunnel kept going for some distance
隧道继续延伸了一段距离

and then the path suddenly dipped down
然后小路突然下降了
Alice had not a moment to think about stopping herself
爱丽丝没有片刻想阻止自己
she found herself falling down and down and down
她发现自己跌倒了，跌倒了，跌倒了
it seemed as if she had fallen down a very deep well
她好像掉进了一口很深的井里
Either the well was very deep, or she fell very slowly
要么井很深，要么她下得很慢
because she had plenty of time to fall
因为她有足够的时间跌倒
as she was falling she could look all around her
当她坠落时，她可以环顾四周
First, she tried to make out where she was going
首先，她试图弄清楚她要去哪里
but the well was too dark to see anything
但井太黑了，什么也看不见
then she looked at the sides of the well
然后她看了看井的两侧
and she noticed that there were cupboards all around her
她注意到她周围到处都是橱柜
and all around the well were book-shelves
井周围都是书架
here and there she saw maps and pictures hung upon pegs
她到处都能看到钉子上挂着的地图和图片
She took down a jar from one of the shelves as she passed
她经过时从其中一个架子上取下了一个罐子
the jar was labelled for its content
这个罐子的内容物被贴上了标签
"MARMALADE MADE FROM ORANGES"
 "橙子做的果酱"
but, to her great disappointment, the marmalade jar was
empty

但是，令她非常失望的是，果酱罐子里是空的
she did not want to drop the empty marmalade jar
她不想掉下空的果酱罐
and her fall was very slow
她的坠落非常缓慢
so she managed to put the marmalade jar into one of the cupboards
所以她设法把果酱罐子放进了一个橱柜里
Down, down, down she fall!
她倒下，倒下，倒下！
Would the fall ever come to an end?
堕落会结束吗？
There was nothing else to do
别无他法
so Alice soon began talking to herself
所以爱丽丝很快就开始自言自语了
"Dinah will miss me very much tonight, I should think!"
“我想，黛娜今晚会非常想我！”
Dinah was Alice's cat
黛娜是爱丽丝的猫
"I hope they'll remember her saucer of milk at tea-time"
“我希望他们会记得她在下午茶时间的牛奶碟”
"Dinah, my dear, I wish you were down here with me!"
“黛娜，亲爱的，我真希望你和我在一起！”
Alice felt that she was dozing off
爱丽丝觉得自己在打瞌睡
and then suddenly, thump! thump!
然后突然，砰的一声！扑通！
down she fell upon a heap of sticks
她倒在了一堆树枝上
and she landed on a pile of dry leaves
她落在一堆干树叶上
and finally the long fall down the hole was over
终于，漫长的坠落结束了

Alice was not a bit hurt
爱丽丝没有受伤
and she jumped up within a moment
她一下子就跳了起来
She looked up, but it was all dark overhead
她抬起头，但头顶上一片漆黑
in front of her was another long corridor
在她面前是另一条长长的走廊
and the White Rabbit was still in sight
而白兔还在眼前
he was hurrying down the corridor
他正匆匆忙忙地沿着走廊走去
There was not a moment to be lost
没有一刻可以浪费
off ran Alice like the wind
爱丽丝像风一样跑了
around the corner turned the rabbit
拐角处转过了兔子
she was just in time to hear the rabbit
她正好听到兔子的声音
""Oh, my ears and whiskers"
	"" 哦，我的耳朵和胡须"
"how late it's getting!"
	"多晚啊！"
She was close behind the rabbit
她紧跟在兔子后面
she turned around another corner
她转过另一个拐角
but the Rabbit was no longer to be seen
但兔子已经不见了
She found herself in a long, low hall
她发现自己在一个又长又低的大厅里
the hall was lit up by a row of ceiling lamps
大厅里有一排吊灯照亮

There were doors all around the hall
大厅周围都是门
but all the doors were locked
但所有的门都锁上了
she walked all the way down one side of the hall
她一路走到大厅的一侧
and she had walked all the way up the other side of the hall
她一路走到大厅的另一边
she had tried every door
她尝试了每一扇门
and she walked sadly down the middle of the hall
她悲伤地走在大厅中间
"how am I ever going to get out again?"
　“我怎么能再出去呢？”

Suddenly she came upon a little table

突然，她来到一张小桌子前

the table was made entirely of solid glass

桌子完全由实心玻璃制成

There was nothing on the table but a tiny golden key

桌子上除了一把小小的金钥匙外什么都没有

the key might belong to one of the doors!

钥匙可能属于其中一扇门！

but, alas! some of the locks were too large for the keys

但是，唉！有些锁对于钥匙来说太大了

and for the other locks the key was too small

而其他锁的钥匙太小了

but, at any rate, the key opened none of the doors

但是，无论如何，钥匙没有打开任何一扇门

but what was she to do?

但她该怎么办呢？

she went through the hall again

她又穿过了大厅

and this time she noticed a low curtain

这一次，她注意到一个低矮的窗帘

behind the curtain was a little door

窗帘后面是一扇小门

the door was about fifteen inches high

门大约有 15 英寸高

She tried the little golden key in the lock

她试了试锁里的小金钥匙

and to her great delight, the key fit in the lock!

令她非常高兴的是，钥匙了锁里！

Alice opened the door

爱丽丝打开了门

and she found the door led into a small corridor

她发现门通向一条小走廊

the corridor was not much larger than a rat-hole

走廊比一个老鼠洞大不了多少
she knelt down and looked along the corridor
她跪下来，沿着走廊看去
and she saw the loveliest garden you have ever seen
她看到了你所见过的最美丽的花园
how she longed to get out of that dark hall
她多么渴望走出那个黑暗的大厅
how she wanted to wander among those bright flowers
她多么想在那些鲜艳的花朵中徜徉
how cool refreshing those fountains looked
刷新那些喷泉看起来多么酷
but she could not even get her head through the doorway
但她甚至无法将头从门口探出
"Oh," said Alice, mournfully
“哦，” 爱丽丝悲哀地说
"how I wish I could fold up like a telescope!"
“我多么希望我能像望远镜一样折叠起来！”
"I think I could fold up like a telescope"
“我觉得我可以像望远镜一样折叠起来”
"if I only knew how to begin"
“如果我知道如何开始”
Alice went back to the table
爱丽丝回到桌子旁
there was the chance of finding another key
有机会找到另一把钥匙
or there might be a book of rules
或者可能有一本规则书
the book could tell her how to fold up like a telescope
这本书可以告诉她如何像望远镜一样折叠起来
This time she found a little bottle
这一次她找到了一个小瓶子
"this bottle certainly was not here before," said Alice
“这瓶酒以前肯定没出现过，” 爱丽丝说
and tied around the neck of the bottle was a paper label

瓶子的脖子上系着一个纸质标签
the label was beautifully printed in large letters
标签上印着精美的大字
"DRINK ME"
"喝我"
"No, I'll look first," she said
"不，我先看看，" 她说
"I'll see whether the bottle is marked as poisonous or not,"
"我看看瓶子是不是被标记为有毒的。"
because she never forgot the lesson about poison
因为她从未忘记关于毒药的教训
"if a bottle is labelled poisonous, it's bound to disagree with you"
"如果一个瓶子被贴上了有毒的标签，它肯定会不同意你的看法"
However, this bottle was not marked as poisonous
然而，这个瓶子并没有被标记为有毒
so Alice ventured to taste the content of the bottle
于是爱丽丝冒险尝尝了瓶子里的东西
she found the liquid quite to her liking
她发现这种液体很合她的胃口
the drink had a sort of mixed flavour
这种饮料有一种混合的味道
cherry-tart, custard, and pineapple
樱桃馅饼、奶油冻和菠萝
roast turkey, toffee, and toast with hot butter
烤火鸡、太妃糖和热黄油吐司
and she soon finished off the bottle
她很快就喝光了这瓶酒
"What a curious feeling!" said Alice
"多么奇怪的感觉啊！"
"I am folding up like a telescope!"
"我像望远镜一样折叠起来！"
And she was folding up like a telescope indeed!

她果然像望远镜一样折叠起来！
She was now only ten inches high
她现在只有十英寸高
and her face brightened up at her thoughts
她的脸因她的思绪而变得明亮起来
now she was the the right size for the little door
现在她的大小正好适合那扇小门
now she could go into that lovely garden
现在她可以走进那个可爱的花园了
soon she stopped getting smaller
很快她就不再变小了
she decided on going into the garden at once
她决定马上进花园
but, alas for poor Alice!
但是，可怜的爱丽丝可惜！
she got to the door
她到了门口
but she had forgotten the little golden key
可是她忘了那把小金钥匙
she went back to the table for the key
她回到桌子前拿钥匙
but she found she could not reach high enough
但她发现自己够不着
she could see the key quite plainly through the glass
她可以透过玻璃清楚地看到钥匙
she tried to climb up the legs of the table
她试图爬上桌腿
but the glass was far too slippery
但玻璃太滑了
eventually she tired herself out with trying
最终，她尝试了一下，让自己疲惫不堪
and the poor little girl sat down and cried
可怜的小女孩坐下来哭泣
Alice spoke to herself rather sharply

爱丽丝对自己说得相当尖锐

"Come, there's no use in crying like that!"

"来，这样哭也没用！"

"I advise you to stop right this minute!"

"我劝你马上停下来！"

She generally gave herself very good advice

她通常给自己很好的建议

though she very seldom followed her own advice

虽然她很少听从自己的建议

and she sometimes was too harsh on herself

她有时对自己太苛刻了

and her words brought tears into her eyes

她的话让她热泪盈眶

Soon her eye fell upon a little glass box

很快，她的目光落在了一个小玻璃盒上

the little glass box was lying under the table

那个小玻璃盒子躺在桌子下面

in the glass box was a very small cake

玻璃盒里有一个非常小的蛋糕

on the cake some words were beautifully written

在蛋糕上，有些文字写得很漂亮

the words had been marked in currants

这些字已经用醋栗标记了

"EAT ME"

"吃我"

"Well, I'll eat the cake," said Alice

"好吧，我来吃蛋糕，" 爱丽丝说

"and if the cake makes me grow larger, I can reach the key"

"如果蛋糕让我长大，我就能拿到钥匙"

"and if the cake makes me grow smaller, I can creep under the door"

"如果蛋糕让我变小了，我就可以悄悄地躲进门下。"

"so either way I'll get into the garden"

　　"所以不管怎样，我都得进花园去。"
"and I don't care which of the two happens!"
　　"而且我不在乎这两种情况中哪一种发生！"
She ate a little bit of the cake
她吃了一点蛋糕
and she anxiously spoke to herself:
她焦急地对自己说：
"Which way? Which way?"
　　"哪条路？哪条路？"
and she held her hand on her head
她把手放在头上
she wanted to feel which way she was growing
她想感受一下自己正在成长的方向
she was quite surprised to find what had happened
她很惊讶地发现发生了什么
she had remained the same size!
她还是一样的大小！
so this time she doubled her efforts
所以这一次她加倍努力
and soon she finished off the whole cake
很快她就吃完了整个蛋糕

The Pool of Tears
泪池

"This is getting more and more interesting!" cried Alice

“这越来越有趣了！”

You can see she was very surprised

你可以看到她非常惊讶

"I'm opening out like the largest telescope there ever was!"

“我像有史以来最大的望远镜一样打开！”

"Good-bye, feet! Oh, my poor little feet"

“再见，脚！哦，我可怜的小脚丫”

"I wonder who will put on your shoes for you now, dears?"

“我想知道现在谁来为你穿鞋呢，亲爱的？”

"and I wonder who will put on your stockings?"

“我想知道谁来穿你的丝袜呢？”

"I shall be a great deal too far away"

“我离得太远了”

"I won't be able trouble myself about you anymore"

“我再也不能为你烦恼了”

Just at this moment her head struck against something

就在这时，她的头撞到了什么东西上

she had reached the roof of the hall

她已经到了大厅的屋顶上

in fact, she was now more than two meters tall

事实上，她现在已经有两米多高了

and she at once took up the little golden key

她立刻拿起了那把小金钥匙

and she hurried off to the garden door

她匆匆忙忙地走到花园门口

Poor Alice! There was not much she could do

可怜的爱丽丝！她能做的不多

she laid down on one side

她躺在一边

and she looked through into the garden with one eye

她用一只眼睛望向花园里

but to get through was more hopeless than ever
但要通过比以往任何时候都更加绝望
She sat down and began to cry again
她坐下来，又开始哭泣
She went on shedding gallons of tears
她继续流泪
soon there was a large pool all around her
很快，她周围就出现了一个大水池
and the water reached half-way down the hall
水已经到了大厅的一半
After a time, she heard a little pattering of feet
过了一会儿，她听到了一点点脚步声
she heard the feet coming from the distance
她听到远处传来的脚步声
and she hastily dried her eyes to see what was coming
她急忙擦干眼睛，看看会发生什么
It was the White Rabbit returning
是白兔回来了
he was splendidly dressed
他穿着华丽
he had a pair of white gloves in one hand
他一只手拿着一双白手套
and he had a large feather fan in the other hand
他的另一只手里拿着一把大羽扇
He came trotting along in a great hurry
他匆匆忙忙地小跑着来
and he muttered to himself, "Oh! the Duchess, the Duchess!"
他喃喃自语道："哦！公爵夫人，公爵夫人！
"Oh! won't she be savage if I've kept her waiting!"
"哦！如果我让她久等，她岂不是很野蛮吗？

When the Rabbit came near her, Alice spoke
当兔子走近她时，爱丽丝开口了
but she spoke in a low, timid voice
但她用低沉而胆怯的声音说话
"sir, please stop what you're doing for one moment"
"先生，请暂时停止您正在做的事情"
The Rabbit startled violently
兔子猛地吓了一跳
he dropped the white gloves and the feather fan
他丢下了白手套和羽毛扇
and he scurried away into the darkness as fast as he could
他以最快的速度跑进了黑暗中
Alice picked up the feather fan and gloves
爱丽丝拿起羽毛扇和手套
and she kept fanning herself while she kept talking
她一边说话一边不停地给自己扇风
"Dear, dear! How strange everything is today!"
"亲爱的，亲爱的！今天的一切都多么奇怪啊！
"yesterday things went on just as usual"

"昨天一切照常进行"

"Was I the same when I got up this morning?"

"我今天早上起床时还是一样吗？"

"But if I'm not the same, there is another question"

"但是如果我不一样，还有另一个问题"

"Who in the world am I?"

"我到底是谁？"

"Ah, that's the great puzzle!"

"啊，这真是个大谜题！"

As she said this, she looked down at her hands

"说这话时，她低头看着自己的手

she was wearing one of the rabbits little white gloves

她戴着一只兔子的小白手套

she hadn't noticed she put the glove on while talking

她没有注意到她在说话时戴上了手套

"How can I have done that?" she thought

"我怎么能那样做呢？"

"I must be growing small again"

"我一定又长大了"

She got up and went to the table to measure her height

她站起来，走到桌子前测量自己的身高

she found that she was now about half a meter tall

她发现自己现在已经有半米左右高了

and she was still shrinking rapidly

她还在迅速地缩小

She soon found out what the cause of the shrinking was

她很快就发现了缩小的原因

the feather fan was making her smaller again!

羽扇又把她弄小了！

and she dropped the feather fan hastily

她匆匆放下了羽扇

she dropped the feather fan just in time to save herself

她及时放下了羽扇，救了自己

had she fanned herself any longer she would have shrunk

away entirely
如果她再给自己扇风，她就会完全缩起来
"That was a narrow escape!" said Alice
　“那真是一次险些逃脱！”
and she was a good deal frightened at the sudden change
她对这突如其来的变化感到非常害怕
but she was very glad to find herself still in existence
但她很高兴发现自己还活着
"And now, off to the garden!"
　“现在，去花园吧！”
And she ran with all speed back to the little door
　“她飞快地跑回那扇小门
but, alas! the little door was shut again
但是，唉！小门又关上了
and the little golden key was lying on the glass table again
小金钥匙又躺在玻璃桌上
"Things are worse than ever," thought the poor child
　“情况比以前更糟了，”这个可怜的孩子想
"I never was so small as this before, never!"
　“我以前从来没有这么小过，从来没有！”
As she said these words, her foot slipped
当她说这些话时，她的脚滑了一下
and in another moment there was a great splash!
又过了一会儿，一阵巨大的水花飞溅起来！
she was up to her chin in salt-water
她在盐水中一直到下巴
Her first idea was that she had somehow fallen into the sea
她的第一个想法是她不知怎么掉进了海里
However, she soon realized what she was in
然而，她很快就意识到了自己的处境
she was in a pool of tears
她泪流满面
the tears she had wept when she was two meters tall
她在两米高时流下的眼泪

Just then she heard something
就在这时，她听到了什么
something was splashing about in the pool
有什么东西在池子里飞溅
the splashing came from a little way off
飞溅的声音来自不远的地方
and she swam nearer to see what the splashing was
她游近了，想看看溅起的水花是什么
she soon saw that it was only a little mouse
她很快就发现那只是一只小老鼠
the little mouse had slipped in to the water too
小老鼠也滑进了水里
Alice thought to herself about the situation
爱丽丝心里想着当时的情况
"Would it be of any use to speak to this mouse?"
“跟这只老鼠说话有什么用吗？”
"Everything is so up-side-down down here"
“这里的一切都是如此颠倒”
"I should think very likely this mouse can talk"

"我觉得这只老鼠很可能会说话"
"at any rate, there's no harm in trying"
"无论如何，尝试一下也没什么坏处"
So she began trying to talk to the mouse
所以她开始尝试与老鼠交谈
"Oh Mouse, do you know the way out of this pool?"
"哦，老鼠，你知道这个池子的出路吗？"
"I am very tired of swimming about here, Oh Mouse!"
"我在这里游来游去已经很累了，哦，老鼠！"
The mouse looked at her rather inquisitively
老鼠好奇地看着她
the mouse seemed to wink with one of its little eyes
老鼠似乎用它的一只小眼睛眨了眨眼
but the little mouse said nothing
可是小老鼠什么也没说
"Perhaps the mouse doesn't understand English," thought Alice
"也许老鼠不懂英语，" 爱丽丝想
"I dare say it's a French mouse"
"我敢说这是一只法国老鼠"
"perhaps this mouse came over with William the Conqueror"
"也许这只老鼠是和征服者威廉一起过来的。"
So she began again, in French
于是她又用法语开始了
"Where is my cat?" she asked in French
她用法语问道： "我的猫在哪里？
it was the first sentence in her French lesson-book
这是她法语课本上的第一句话
The Mouse gave a sudden leap out of the water
老鼠突然从水里跳了出来
and the mouse seemed to quiver all over with fright
老鼠似乎吓得浑身颤抖
"Oh, I beg your pardon!" cried Alice hastily
"噢，我求你原谅！"

she was afraid that she had hurt the poor animal's feelings
她害怕自己伤害了这只可怜的动物的感情
"I quite forgot you didn't like cats"
　“我真忘了你不喜欢猫”
"I don't like cats!" cried the Mouse in a shrill, passionate voice
　“我不喜欢猫！” 　老鼠用尖锐而热情的声音喊道
"Would you like cats, if you were me?"
　“如果你是我，你想要猫吗？”
Alice comforted the mouse in a soothing tone
爱丽丝用安抚的语气安慰老鼠
"Well, perhaps I would not like cats if I were you either"
　“嗯，如果我是你，也许我也不喜欢猫”
"please don't be angry about the mention of cats"
　“请不要因为提到猫而生气”
"And yet I wish I could show you our cat Dinah"
　“但我希望我能带你看看我们的猫黛娜”
"if you met her I think you'd take a fancy to cats"
　“如果你遇见她，我想你会喜欢猫”
"if you could only see her"
　“如果你能看到她就好了”
"She is such a dear, quiet thing"
　“她是个如此可爱、安静的东西”
The mouse was shaking all over
老鼠浑身颤抖
Alice felt certain the mouse must be really offended
爱丽丝确信这只老鼠一定是真的被冒犯了
"We won't talk about her any more, if you'd rather not"
　“如果你愿意的话，我们不会再谈论她了”
"We, indeed!" cried the Mouse
　“我们，真的！”
the mouse was trembling down to the end of its tail
老鼠颤抖着，一直到尾巴的末端
"As if I would talk on such a subject!"

"好像我会谈论这样的话题一样！"
"Our family always hated cats"
"我们家一直都讨厌猫"
"cats; nasty, low, vulgar things!"
"猫；、低级、粗俗的东西！"
"Don't let me hear the name again!"
"别让我再听到这个名字！"
"I won't mention cats again indeed!" said Alice
"我真的不会再提猫了！"
she was in a great hurry to change the subject
她急着要转移话题
"Are you... are you fond of dogs?"
"你是……你喜欢狗吗？
"There is such a nice little dog near our house,"
"我们家附近有一只这么漂亮的小狗，"
"I should like to show you the little dog!"
"我想带你看看那只小狗！"
"this little dog kills all the rats and...
"这只小狗杀死了所有的老鼠，然后……
"oh, dear!" cried Alice in a sorrowful tone
"噢，亲爱的！" 爱丽丝用悲哀的语气叫道
"I'm afraid I've offended you again!"
"恐怕又得罪你了！"
the mouse was swimming away from her as fast as it could go
老鼠以最快的速度从她身边游走
and the mouse made quite a commotion in the pool
老鼠在池子里引起了不小的骚动
So she called softly after the mouse
于是她轻声地追着老鼠叫了一声
"my dear mouse, please come back!"
"我亲爱的老鼠，请回来！"
"and we won't talk about cats"
"我们不会谈论猫"

"and we don't have to talk about dogs either"
"我们也不必谈论狗"
When the mouse heard this, it turned around
老鼠听到这话，转过身来
and the little mouse swam slowly back to her
小老鼠慢慢地游回她身边
the mouse's face was quite pale
老鼠的脸色很苍白
and the mouse spoke, in a low, trembling voice
老鼠用低沉、颤抖的声音说话
"Let us get to the shore"
"我们到岸边去"
"and then I'll tell you my history"
"然后我会告诉你我的历史"
"and you'll understand why it is I hate cats and dogs"
"你就会明白为什么我讨厌猫和狗了"
It had become high time to go
现在是该走的时候了
because the pool was getting quite crowded
因为游泳池变得非常拥挤
other birds and animals had fallen into the pool
其他鸟类和动物也掉进了水池里
there were a Duck and a Dodo
有一只鸭子和一只渡渡鸟
and there was a Lory bird and an Eaglet
还有一只 Lory 鸟和一只 Eaglet
and there were several other interesting looking creatures
还有其他几个看起来很有趣的生物
Alice led the way out the pool
爱丽丝带路走出了游泳池
and the whole party of animals swam to the shore
于是，一队动物都游到了岸边

A caucus race and a long tail
预选会议和长尾巴

They were indeed a funny-looking bunch of animals
他们确实是一群看起来很滑稽的动物
and they all assembled on the water's bank
他们都聚集在水岸上
the birds all had bedraggled feathers
鸟儿的羽毛都破烂不堪
and the furry animals were soaked through
毛茸茸的动物被浸透了
and all were dripping wet, annoyed and uncomfortable
所有人都湿漉漉的，恼火和不舒服

there was one question that had to be answered first
首先必须回答一个问题
what is the best way for everyone to get dry?
大家擦干的最佳方式是什么？
They had a consultation about this matter
他们就此事进行了磋商
soon they were all on familiar terms

很快他们就熟悉了

it was as if she had known them all her life

就好像她一辈子都认识他们一样

the mouse seemed to be a person of some authority

老鼠似乎是一个有权威的人

"Sit down, all of you, and listen to me!"

“你们都坐下，听我说！”

"I'll soon make you all dry again!"

“我很快就会让你们都干的！”

They all sat down at once, in a large ring

他们同时围成一圈坐下

and the little mouse sat in the middle

小老鼠坐在中间

"Ahem!" said the mouse with an important air

“咳咳！”

"Are you all ready?"

“你们都准备好了吗？”

"This is the driest thing I know"

“这是我所知道的最干燥的事情”

"Silence all around, if you please!"

“如果你愿意的话，周围安静！”

"William the Conqueror was favoured by the pope"

“征服者威廉受到教皇的青睐”

"but he was soon submitted to by the English"

“但他很快就被英国人臣服了”

"they wanted leaders of late"

“他们想要最近的领导人”

"and they had been accustomed to power and conquest"

“他们已经习惯了权力和征服”

"Edwin and Morcar, the Earls of Mercia and Northumbria"

“埃德温和莫尔卡，麦西亚伯爵和诺森比亚伯爵”

"Ugh!" said the lori bird, with a shiver

“呃，”那只萝莉鸟说，打了个寒颤

"and even Stigand, the patriotic archbishop of Canterbury"

"甚至还有爱国的坎特伯雷大主教斯蒂甘德"
"he also found it advisable"
"他也觉得这是可取的"
"What did he find advisable?" said the duck
"他觉得什么好呢？"
"He found it advisable" the mouse replied rather crossly
"他觉得这是可取的，" 老鼠相当生气地回答
but the duck was not satisfied
但鸭子并不满意
"of course, you know what 'it' means"
"当然，你知道'它'是什么意思"
"I know what 'it' is when I find a thing," said the duck
"当我找到一个东西时，我就知道'它'是什么，" 鸭子说
"it's generally a frog or a worm"
"它通常是青蛙或蠕虫"
"The question is, what did the archbishop find?"
"问题是，大主教发现了什么？"
The mouse did not notice this question
鼠标没有注意到这个问题
instead, the mouse hurriedly went on with the speech
相反，老鼠匆匆忙忙地继续演讲
"he found it advisable to go with Edgar Atheling"
"他觉得和埃德加·阿瑟林一起去是明智的。"
"to meet William and offer him the crown"
"去见威廉，把王冠献给他"
the mouse continued, turning to Alice as it spoke
老鼠继续说着，一边转向爱丽丝
"How are you getting on now, my dear?"
"你现在怎么样了，亲爱的？"
"As wet as ever," said Alice in a melancholy tone
"一如既往地湿漉漉的，" 爱丽丝用忧郁的语气说
"this story doesn't seem to dry me at all"
"这个故事似乎一点也不让我感到干燥"

"In that case," said the dodo solemnly, rising to its feet

　"既然如此，" 渡渡鸟严肃地说，站了起来

"I vote that the meeting be adjourned"

　"我投票决定休会"

"and I propose an immediate adoption of more energetic remedies"

　"我建议立即采用更有力的补救措施"

"Speak real words!" said the eaglet

　"说真话！"

"I don't know the meaning of half of those long words"

　"我不知道那些长词的一半是什么意思"

"and, what's more, I don't believe you know either!"

　"而且，我不相信你也知道！"

"What I was going to say," said the dodo in an offended tone

　"我本来想说的，" 渡渡鸟用一种被冒犯的语气说

"the best thing to get us dry would be a caucus-race"

　"让我们干涸的最好办法是预选会议"

"What is a caucus-race?" said Alice

　"什么是预选会议？"

"Well," said the dodo, "the best way to explain it is to do it"
"嗯，"渡渡鸟说，"最好的解释方式就是去做。
"First the dodo marked out a race-course"
"首先，渡渡鸟划定了一个赛马路线"
"the track was in a sort of circle"
"轨道在某种圆圈中"
"and then all the party were placed along the course"
"然后所有的队伍都沿着路线布置。"
There was no "One, two, three and away!"
没有"一、二、三和远！
but they began running when they liked
但他们想跑就跑
and they also finished when they liked
他们也想什么时候结束就结束
so it was not easy to know when the race was over
因此，要知道比赛何时结束并不容易
after half an hour or so of running they were all quite dry
跑了半个小时左右后，他们都已经干了
the dodo suddenly called out, "The race is over!"
渡渡鸟突然喊道："比赛结束了！
and they all crowded around the dodo
他们都挤在渡渡鸟周围
all the animals were panting and puffing
所有的动物都在喘气和喘气
and they all wanted to know, "But who has won?"
他们都想知道，"但谁赢了？
This question the dodo could not immediately answer
这个问题渡渡鸟无法立即回答
first he had to do a great deal of thinking
首先，他必须做大量的思考
after much thinking, the dodo finally spoke
经过深思熟虑，渡渡鸟终于开口了
"Everybody has won, and all must have prizes"
"每个人都赢了，而且所有人都必须有奖品"

"But who is to give the prizes?" asked a chorus of voices
"可是，谁来颁奖呢？"
"Well, she, of course," said the dodo
"嗯，她，当然，" 渡渡鸟说
and the dodo pointed with one finger to Alice
渡渡鸟用一根手指指向爱丽丝
and the whole party of animals crowded around her
还有一大群动物都挤在她周围
they called out, in a confused way, "Prizes! Prizes!"
他们困惑地喊道："奖品！奖品！
Alice had no idea what to do
爱丽丝不知道该怎么办
in despair she put her hand into her pocket
绝望中，她把手伸进口袋里
and she pulled out a box of sweets
她拿出一盒糖果
luckily the salt-water had not got into the box
幸运的是，盐水没有进入箱子
and she handed the sweets around as prizes
她把糖果当奖品递给大家
There was exactly one piece for everyone
每个人都有一件
The next thing they had to do was to eat the sweets
他们接下来要做的是吃糖果
this caused some noise and confusion
这引起了一些噪音和混乱
the large birds complained that they could not taste their sweets
大鸟抱怨它们尝不到自己的甜食
the small ones choked and had to be patted on the back
小的呛住了，不得不拍拍背
However, it was over at last
然而，它终于结束了
and they sat down again in a ring

他们又围成一圈坐下
and they begged the mouse to tell them something more
他们恳求老鼠再告诉他们一些事情
"You promised to tell me your history, you know," said Alice
"你知道的，你答应过要把你的经历告诉我，"爱丽丝说
and she made another little remark about cats in a whisper
她又悄悄地说了一句关于猫的事
she didn't want to offend the mouse again
她不想再得罪老鼠了
the little mouse turned to Alice and sighed
小老鼠转向爱丽丝，叹了口气
"Mine is a long and a sad tale!"
"我的是一个漫长而悲伤的故事！"
"It is a long tail, certainly," said Alice
"当然是一条长尾巴，"爱丽丝说
and she looked down with wonder at the mouse's tail
她惊奇地低头看着老鼠的尾巴
"but why do you call it a sad tail?"
"可是你为什么叫它悲伤的尾巴呢？"
And she kept on puzzling about it while the mouse was speaking
当老鼠说话时，她一直在困惑
so that her idea of the tale was something like this
所以她对这个故事的想法是这样的

"Fury said to
a mouse, That
he met in the
house, 'Let
us both go
to law: *I*
will prosecute
you.—
Come, I'll
take no denial:
We must have
the trial;
For really
this morning
I've
nothing
to do.'
Said the
mouse to
the cur,
'Such a
trial, dear
sir, With
no jury
or judge,
would
be wasting
our
breath.'
'I'll be
judge,
I'll be
jury,'
said
cunning
old
Fury;
'I'll
try
the
whole
cause,
and
condemn
you to
death.'"

Fury said to a mouse, That he met in the house"
弗瑞对一只老鼠说，他在房子里遇见了。
Let us both go to law: I will prosecute you
让我们俩都去打官司：我会起诉你
Come, I'll take no denial: We must have the trial
来吧，我不会否认：我们必须接受审判
For really this morning I've nothing to do
因为今天早上我真的无事可做
Said the mouse to the cur;
老鼠对着诅咒说；

Such a trial, dear sir, With no jury or judge, would be wasting our breath

这样的审判，亲爱的先生，没有陪审团或法官，简直是浪费我们的呼吸

"I'll be judge, I'll be jury," said cunning old Fury

"我来当法官，我来当陪审团，"狡猾的老弗瑞说

I'll try the whole cause, and condemn you to death

我要把整个案子都试一遍，把你判死刑

the mouse spoke severely to Alice

老鼠对爱丽丝严厉地说话

"You are not paying attention!"

"你没注意！"

"What are you thinking of?"

"你在想什么？"

"I beg your pardon," said Alice very humbly

"请原谅，"爱丽丝非常谦虚地说

"you had got to the fifth bend, I think?"

"我想你已经到了第五个弯道吧？"

"You insult me by talking such nonsense!"

"你说这种废话，侮辱我！"

and the mouse got up and walked away

老鼠起身走开了

Alice called after the little mouse

爱丽丝在小老鼠后面喊道

"Please come back and finish your story!"

"请回来把你的故事讲完！"

And the others all joined in chorus

其他人也都加入了合唱

"Yes, please do finish your story!"

"是的，请把你的故事讲完！"

But the mouse only shook its head impatiently

但老鼠只是不耐烦地摇了摇头

and the little mouse walked a little quicker

小老鼠走得更快了

"I wish I had Dinah, our cat, here!" said Alice
“我真希望我们的猫黛娜在这里！”
This caused a remarkable sensation among the party
这在党内引起了非凡的轰动
Some of the birds hurried off at once
一些鸟儿立刻匆匆走了
and a Canary called out in a trembling voice, to its children;
一只金丝雀用颤抖的声音向它的孩子们喊道；
"Come away, my dears!"
“走开，亲爱的！”
"It's high time you were all in bed!"
“你们都该躺在床上了！”
with various excuses they all went away
他们找了各种借口都走了
and Alice was soon left alone
爱丽丝很快就独自一人
"I wish I hadn't mentioned Dinah!"
“我真希望我没有提到黛娜！”
"Nobody seems to like her down here"
“这里似乎没有人喜欢她”
"but I'm sure she's the best cat in the world!"
“但我敢肯定她是世界上最好的猫！”
Poor Alice began to cry again
可怜的爱丽丝又开始哭泣了
because she felt very lonely and low-spirited
因为她感到非常孤独和低落
In a little while, however, she again heard something
然而，过了一会儿，她又听到了什么
a little pattering of footsteps in the distance
远处传来轻微的脚步声
and she looked up eagerly
她急切地抬起头来

The rabbit sends in little Mr Bill
兔子送来了小比尔先生

It was the white rabbit,trotting slowly back again
是那只白兔，又慢慢地小跑回来了
he was looking about anxiously as he went
他一边走一边焦急地四处张望
he looked as if he had lost something
他看起来好像丢了什么东西
Alice heard him muttering to himself
爱丽丝听见他喃喃自语
"The Duchess! The Duchess! Oh, my dear paws!"
"公爵夫人！公爵夫人！哦，我亲爱的爪子！
"Oh, my fur and whiskers!"
"哦，我的皮毛和胡须！"
"She'll get me executed, I'm sure of that"
"她会把我处死的，我很确定"
"just as sure as ferrets are ferrets!"
"就像雪貂就是雪貂一样！"
"Where can I have dropped my things, I wonder?"
"我想知道，我能把我的东西丢在哪里？"
Alice guessed in a moment what he was looking for
爱丽丝瞬间猜到了他在找什么
he was looking for the feather fan

他在找羽扇
and he was looking for the pair of white gloves
他正在寻找那双白手套
so she very good-naturedly began looking for the gloves
所以她非常善良地开始寻找手套
and she looked for the feather fan too
她也找了羽扇
but the gloves and feather fan were nowhere to be seen
但手套和羽扇却无处可寻
everything seemed to have changed since her swim in the pool
自从她在游泳池里游泳以来，一切似乎都发生了变化
nothing was the same since she had been in the great hall
自从她在大厅里以来，一切都不一样了
and the glass table had vanished
玻璃桌也不见了
and the little door wasn't there either
而且那扇小门也不在那里
Very soon the rabbit noticed Alice
很快，兔子就注意到了爱丽丝
he called to her in an angry tone
他用愤怒的语气呼唤她
"Mary Ann, what are you doing out here?"
"Mary Ann，你在这儿做什么？"
"Run home this moment"
"这一刻跑回家"
"and fetch me a pair of gloves and a feather fan!"
"给我拿一双手套和一把羽扇来！"
"and be quick about it!"
"而且要快点！"
Alice spoke to herself as she ran off
爱丽丝一边跑一边自言自语
"He must have mistaken me for his housemaid!"
"他一定把我误认为是他的女仆了！"

"How surprised he'll be when he finds out who I am!"
"当他发现我是谁时，他会多么惊讶啊！"
As she said this, she came upon a neat little house
"说这话的时候，她来到了一座整洁的小房子里
on the door of the house was a bright brass plate
房子的门上挂着一块亮丽的铜牌
"W. RABBIT"
"W．兔"
She went in without knocking on the door
她没有敲门就进去了
and she hurried straight upstairs
她急忙径直上楼
she worried that she might meet the real Mary Ann
她担心自己可能会遇到真正的玛丽安
because then she would be turned out of the house
因为那样她就会被赶出家门
and she wouldn't be able to find the feather fan and gloves
而且她找不到羽扇和手套
Alice had found her way into a tidy little room
爱丽丝走进了一个整洁的小房间
in the room was a table by the window
房间里靠窗有一张桌子
and on the table was a feather fan
桌子上放着一把羽毛扇
and there were two or three pairs of tiny white gloves
还有两三双小白手套
she picked up the feather fan and a pair of the gloves
她拿起了羽扇和一双手套
and she was just about to leave the room
她正要离开房间
but then her eyes fell upon a little bottle
但随后她的目光落在了一个小瓶子上
She uncorked the bottle and put it to her lips
她打开瓶子的瓶塞，把它放在嘴唇上

"I do hope it'll make me grow large again"
"我真心希望它能让我再次长大"
"I'm tired of being such a tiny little thing!"
"我受够了做这么小东西！"
Alice had hardly drunk half the bottle
爱丽丝几乎没喝完半瓶
her head was already pressing against the ceiling
她的头已经压在天花板上
and she had to stoop down
她不得不弯下腰
to save her neck from being broken
为了不让她的脖子被折断
She hastily put down the bottle
她匆匆放下了瓶子
"That's quite enough"
"这就够了"
"I hope I don't grow anymore"
"我希望我不要再长大了"
Alas! It was too late to wish that!
唉！希望那已经太晚了！
She went on growing and growing
她不断成长
and very soon she had to kneel down on the floor
很快她就不得不跪在地板上
and even then she went on growing
即便如此，她还是继续成长
as a last resource she put one arm out of the window
作为最后的资源，她把一只手臂伸出窗外
and she put one foot up the chimney
她把一只脚伸进烟囱里
"Now I can do no more, whatever happens"
"现在我不能再做任何事情了，无论发生什么"
"What will become of me?"
"我会变成什么样子？"

Alice had a spot of luck
爱丽丝有一点运气
the little magic bottle had had its full effect
小魔术瓶已经发挥了它的全部作用
and Alice grew no larger than she was
爱丽丝并没有长得比她大
After a few minutes she heard a voice outside
几分钟后，她听到外面有声音
and she stopped to listen to the voice
她停下来听那声音
"Mary Ann! Mary Ann!" said the voice
"玛丽·安！玛丽安！
"Fetch me my gloves this moment!"
"马上把我的手套拿来！"
Then came a little pattering of feet on the stairs
然后，楼梯上传来了一阵轻微的脚步声
Alice knew it was the rabbit coming to look for her
爱丽丝知道是兔子来找她了
and she trembled till she shook the house
她战战兢兢，直到震动了房子
she quite forgot what her proportions were

她完全忘记了自己的比例是多少
she was a thousand times as large as the rabbit
她比兔子大一千倍
and she had no reason to be afraid of a rabbit
她没有理由害怕兔子
Presently the rabbit came up to the door
不一会儿，兔子走到门口
and the little rabbit tried to open the door
小兔子试图打开门
the door started to open inwards
门开始向内打开
but Alice's elbow was pressed hard against the door
但爱丽丝的胳膊肘被狠狠地压在门上
that attempt proved a failure
那次尝试被证明是失败的
Alice heard the rabbit speak to himself
爱丽丝听到兔子自言自语
"Then I'll go around and get in through the window"
　"那我就绕着走，从窗户进去。"
"That you won't!" thought Alice
　"你不会的！"
and she waited a little again
她又等了一会儿
soon she heard the rabbit just under the window
很快，她就听到了窗下的兔子
she suddenly spread out her hand
她突然伸出手
and she made a snatch in the air
她在空中猛地一把
She did not get hold of anything
她什么也没拿
but she heard a little shriek and a fall
但她听到了一声尖叫和一阵摔倒
and she heard a crash of broken glass

她听到了玻璃碎裂的撞击声
perhaps the rabbit had fallen
也许兔子掉下来了
maybe he was in a green-house
也许他在温室里
Next came an angry voice; the rabbit's voice
接着传来一个愤怒的声音；兔子的声音
"Pat, where are you?"
"Pat，你在哪儿？"
And then came a voice she had never heard before
然后传来了一个她从未听过的声音
"your honour, I'm here!"
"大人，我在这里！"
"I'm digging for apples"
"我在挖苹果"
"Here! Come and help me out of this!"
"来！快来帮我走吧！
"Now tell me, Pat, what's that in the window?"
"现在告诉我，帕特，窗户里有什么？"
"Sure, your honour, I will tell you"
"好的，大人，我会告诉你的。"
"it's an arm that's in the window!"
"这是一只在窗户里的手臂！"
"Well, an arm has no business there"
"嗯，一只手臂在那里没什么用"
"go and take the arm away!"
"去把那条胳膊拿走！"
There was a long silence after this
之后是长时间的沉默
and Alice could only hear whispers now and then
爱丽丝只能时不时地听到耳语
and at last she spread out her hand again
最后，她又伸出了手
and she made another snatch in the air

她又在空中抓了一下

This time there were two little shrieks

这一次传来了两声小小的尖叫

and there was more sounds of broken glass

玻璃破碎的声音越来越大

"I wonder what they'll do next!" thought Alice

“我想知道他们接下来要做什么！”

"I wish they would pull me out the window"

“我希望他们能把我拉出窗外”

She waited for some time

她等了一会儿

but for a while she didn't hear anything more

但有一阵子，她什么也没听到

At last came a rumbling of little wheels

最后，传来了小轮子的隆隆声

and there came the sound of a good many voices

这时传来了许多声音

all the voices were talking together

所有的声音都在一起说话

She could make out some of the words

她能听清一些字

"Where's the other ladder?"

“另一个梯子呢？”

"Bill's got the other ladder"

“比尔有另一个梯子”

"Bill, come here!"

“比尔，过来！”

"Will the roof bear the load?"

“屋顶能承受负载吗？”

"Who wants to go down the chimney?"

“谁想从烟囱里下去？”

"Nay, I shall not! You do it!"

“不，我不会的！你来做吧！

"Here, Bill!"

"来，比尔！"

"The master says you've got to go down the chimney!"

"主人说你得从烟囱下去！"

Alice drew her foot as far down the chimney as she could

爱丽丝把脚尽可能地伸到烟囱里

and then she waited to see what was coming

然后她等着看会发生什么

she heard a little animal scratching and scrambling

她听到一只小动物在抓挠和争吵

the little animal must be in the chimney

小动物一定在烟囱里

then she gave one sharp kick

然后她猛地踢了一脚

and she waited to see what would happen next

她等着看接下来会发生什么

she heard a general chorus of voices

她听到了一阵普遍的合唱

"There goes Bill!" they all said

"比尔走了！"

then she heard the rabbit's voice alone

然后她听到了兔子独自的声音

"You by the hedge, catch him!"

"你在树篱边，抓住他！"

there was another moment of silence

又是一阵沉默

and then there was another confusion of voices

然后又是一阵混乱的声音

"Hold up his head, Brandy"

"抬起他的头，白兰地"

"be careful not to choke him"

"小心不要让他窒息"

"What happened to you?"

"你怎么了？"

Last came a little feeble, squeaking voice

最后传来一个有点微弱、吱吱作响的声音
"Well, I hardly know no more"
　"嗯，我几乎不知道更多了"
"thank you all, I'm better now"
　"谢谢大家，我现在好多了"
"there is one thing I can remember"
　"有一件事我能记住"
"something comes at me like a train in a tunnel"
　"有什么东西像隧道里的火车一样向我袭来"
"and up I fly like a sky-rocket!"
　"我像火箭一样飞起来！"
there was a minute or two of silence
一两分钟的沉默
and then they began moving about again
然后他们又开始四处走动
and Alice heard the Rabbit speak again
爱丽丝又听到兔子说话了
"A barrowful will do, to begin with"
　"一开始，一个 barrowful 就可以了"
"A barrowful of what?" thought Alice
　"什么？"　爱丽丝想
But she was not kept in suspense for long
但她并没有长时间处于悬念中
a shower of little pebbles came through the window
一阵小鹅卵石从窗户里射进来
and some of the little pebbles hit her in the face
一些小鹅卵石打在她的脸上
Alice was surprised about the little pebbles
爱丽丝对这些小鹅卵石感到惊讶
all the little pebbles were turning into cakes
所有的小鹅卵石都变成了蛋糕
and a bright idea came into her head
一个好主意出现在她的脑海中
"I should eat one of these cakes"

"我应该吃其中一个蛋糕"
"cake is sure to make some change in my size"
"蛋糕肯定会改变我的尺码"
So she swallowed one of the cakes
所以她吞下了其中一个蛋糕
and she was delighted to find that she began shrinking
她很高兴地发现自己开始缩小
soon she was small enough to get through the door
很快她就小到可以进门了
she ran out of the house
她跑出了房子
a crowd of little animals and birds were waiting outside
一群小动物和小鸟在外面等着
all the little birds and animals rushed at Alice
所有的小鸟和小动物都向爱丽丝冲来
but she ran off as fast as she could
但她以最快的速度跑开了
and soon she found herself safe in a thick wood
很快，她发现自己在一片茂密的树林里很安全
Alice wandered about in the woods
爱丽丝在树林里徘徊
and she thought to herself:
她心想：
"I know what I have to do first"
"我知道我首先要做什么"
"first I have to grow to my right size again"
"首先，我必须再次长到合适的尺寸"
"and then I have to find my way into that lovely garden"
"然后我得想办法进那个可爱的花园。"
"I suppose I ought to eat or drink something or other"
"我想我应该吃点东西或喝点什么的"
"but the question is what should I eat or drink?"
"但问题是我应该吃什么或喝什么？"
Alice looked all around her at the flowers

爱丽丝环顾四周的花朵
and she looked through the blades of grass
她透过草叶向外望去
but she could not see anything to eat or drink
但她看不到任何可吃的东西或可喝的东西
nothing looked like the right thing to eat or drink
看起来没有什么东西是适合吃或喝的东西
There was a large mushroom growing near her
她附近长着一朵大蘑菇
the mushroom was about the same height as Alice
蘑菇的高度与爱丽丝差不多
She stretched herself up on tiptoes
她踮起脚尖伸展身体
and she peeped over the edge of the mushroom
她从蘑菇的边缘偷看
her eyes immediately met the eyes of a large blue caterpillar
她的眼睛立即与一只蓝色大毛毛虫的眼睛相遇
the caterpillar was sitting on the top of the mushroom
毛毛虫坐在蘑菇的顶部
and the caterpillar had crossed all his arms
毛毛虫已经交叉了他的所有手臂
and he was quietly smoking a long hookah
他静静地抽着一根长长的水烟
and he took not the smallest notice of anything
他丝毫没有注意到任何事情
and he certainly didn't pay attention to Alice
他当然没有注意爱丽丝

Advice from a caterpillar
来自毛毛虫的建议
At last the caterpillar took the hookah out of its mouth
最后，毛毛虫从嘴里把水烟袋拿了出来
and he addressed Alice in a languid, sleepy voice
他用一种慵懒、困倦的声音对爱丽丝说
"Who are you?" said the caterpillar
"你是谁？"

Alice replied, rather shyly, "I hardly know, sir"
爱丽丝相当害羞地回答说："我几乎不知道，先生。
"just at the moment it's all a bit..."
"只是此刻，一切都有点……"
"I know who I was when I got up this morning""
"我知道我今天早上起床时是谁。"
"but I think I must have changed several times since then"
"但我想，从那以后我肯定已经变了好几次了。"
"What do you mean by that?" said the caterpillar
"你这话是什么意思？"
sternly the caterpillar asked her to explain herself

毛毛虫严厉地要求她解释一下
"I can't explain myself, I'm afraid, sir," said Alice
　"恐怕我自己说不清，先生，" 爱丽丝说
"because I'm not myself"
　"因为我不是我自己"
"you see, being so many different sizes in a day is very confusing"
　"你看，一天有这么多不同的尺码是非常令人困惑的
"

She pulled herself up and said very gravely:
她站起来，非常严肃地说：
"I think you ought to tell me who you are, first"
　"我觉得你应该先告诉我你是谁。"
"Why?" said the caterpillar
　"为什么？"
Alice could not think of any good reason
爱丽丝想不出什么好的理由
and the caterpillar seemed to be in a very unpleasant state of mind
毛毛虫似乎处于一种非常不愉快的精神状态
so she turned away
所以她转身离开了
"Come back!" the caterpillar called after her
毛毛虫在她身后喊道
"I've something important to say!"
　"我有重要的事情要说！"
Alice turned and came back again
爱丽丝转过身来，又回来了
"Keep your temper," said the caterpillar
　"保持你的脾气，" 毛毛虫说
"Is that all?" said Alice
　"就这些吗？"
and she swallowed her anger as well as she could
她尽可能地压制住了自己的愤怒

"No," said the caterpillar
"不，"毛毛虫说
the caterpillar unfolded its arms
毛毛虫张开双臂
and he took the hookah out of his mouth again
他又把水烟袋从嘴里拿出来
and he said, "So you think you're changed, do you?"
他说，"所以你觉得你变了，是吗？
"I'm afraid, I am changed, sir," said Alice
"恐怕，我变了，先生，"爱丽丝说
"I can't remember things as I used to remember them"
"我记不住以前记得的事情了"
"and I don't stay the same size for more than ten minutes!"
"而且我不会保持相同的大小超过十分钟！"
"What size do you want to be?" asked the caterpillar
毛毛虫问道："你想变成什么大小？
"Oh, I don't particularly mind what size I am," Alice hastily replied
"哦，我不是特别在意我的体型，"爱丽丝急忙回答
"I just don't like changing size so often, you know"
"我就是不喜欢这么频繁地改变尺码，你知道的"
"I would like to be a little larger, sir"
"我想再大一点，先生"
"if you wouldn't mind," added Alice
"如果你不介意的话，"爱丽丝补充道
"Ten centimetres is such a wretched height to be"
"10 厘米真是太可怕了"
"It is a very good height indeed!" said the caterpillar angrily
"这确实是一个非常好的高度！"
and he reared itself upright as he spoke
他说话的时候站直了身子
he was exactly ten centimetres high
他正好有十厘米高
In a minute or two, the caterpillar got down off the

mushroom
一两分钟后，毛毛虫从蘑菇上下来了
and he crawled away into the grass
他就爬到草地上去了
as he went away, he made some little remarks
他走的时候，说了一些小话
"One side will make you grow taller"
“一侧会让你长高”
"and the other side will make you grow shorter"
“另一边会让你长得矮”
"One side of what?" thought Alice to herself
“一边是什么？” 爱丽丝心想
"The other side of what?"
“另一边是什么？”
"the side of the mushroom," said the caterpillar
“蘑菇的侧面，” 毛毛虫说
it was as if she had asked her question aloud
就好像她大声地问了她的问题一样
and in another moment, he was out of sight
再过一会儿，他就消失在视线中了
Alice remained looking thoughtfully at the mushroom
爱丽丝仍然若有所思地看着蘑菇
she was trying to make out which were the two sides of the mushroom
她试图弄清楚蘑菇的两面是哪一面
At last she stretched her arms around the mushroom
最后，她伸出双臂搂住了蘑菇
and she broke off a bit of the edges
她把边缘掰掉了一点
"And now, which side is which?" she said to herself
“那么现在，哪边是哪边呢？”
and she nibbled a little of the right-hand bit
她啃了一点右手的那块
The next moment she felt a violent blow underneath her

chin
下一刻，她感到下巴下方受到了猛烈的打击
her chin had struck her foot!
她的下巴撞到了她的脚！
She was a good deal frightened by this very sudden change
她被这个非常突然的变化吓坏了
she was shrinking very rapidly
她缩小得非常快
so she quickly ate some of the other bit of mushroom
所以她很快就吃掉了另一块蘑菇
Her chin was pressed very closely against her foot
她的下巴紧紧地压在脚上
there was hardly room to open her mouth
她几乎没有张口的空间
but she did at last manage to open her mouth
但她终于设法张开了嘴
and she swallowed a morsel of the left-hand bit
她吞下了一小口左手的
"my head's been freed at last!" said Alice
“我的头终于被解放出来了！”
she looked down at herself
她低头看着自己
but all she could see was an immense length of neck
但她只能看到一条巨大的脖子
her neck seemed to rise like a stalk
她的脖子似乎像一根茎一样高起
and she looked down over a sea of green leaves
她俯视着一片绿叶的海洋
"Where have my shoulders gotten to?"
“我的肩膀到哪儿去了？”
"And oh, my poor hands, how is it I can't see you?"
“哦，我可怜的手，我怎么看不见你呢？”
but her neck did have one benefit
但她的脖子确实有一个好处

she could move her head in any direction
她可以向任何方向移动她的头
in fact, she was just like a serpent
事实上，她就像一条蛇
she gracefully zigzagged her head down
她优雅地曲折地低下头
and she moved her head through the trees
她把头穿过树林
but then she heard a sharp hiss
但随后她听到了一声尖锐的嘶嘶声
and she quickly pulled her head back
她很快就把头往后拉
a large pigeon had flown into her face
一只大鸽子飞到了她的脸上
and the pigeon was violently with its wings
鸽子猛烈地摆动着翅膀

"Serpent!" cried the pigeon
　“蛇！”
"I'm not a serpent!" said Alice indignantly
　“我不是蛇！”
"Leave me alone!"
　“别管我！”
"I've tried the roots of trees"
　“我试过树根”
"and I've tried hedges," the pigeon went on
　“我试过树篱，” 鸽子继续说
"but those serpents! There's no pleasing them!"
　“可是那些蛇！没有办法取悦他们！
Alice was more and more puzzled
爱丽丝越来越困惑
"As if it wasn't trouble enough hatching the eggs," said the
pigeon
　“好像孵化蛋还不够麻烦，” 鸽子说
"by night and day I must look out for serpents too!"
　“无论白天还是黑夜，我也必须提防蛇！”
"I had just found the highest tree in the forest"
　“我刚刚找到了森林里最高的树”
"surely I'd be free from serpents here?"
　“我在这里肯定不会有蛇吗？”
"and out comes a serpent from the sky!"
　“一条蛇从天上出来！”
"But I'm not a serpent, I tell you!" said Alice
　“可是我告诉你，我不是蛇！”
"I'm a... I'm a... I'm a little girl," she added rather doubtfully
　“我是......我是...我是个小女孩，” “她颇为怀疑
地补充道
she had after all been going through a lot of changes
毕竟，她经历了很多变化
"You're looking for eggs," said the pigeon
　“你在找蛋，” 鸽子说

"I know that for a fact"
“我知道这是事实”
"and what does it matter if you're a little girl or a serpent?"
“那么，你是个小女孩还是一条蛇又有什么关系呢？
”

"It matters a good deal to me," said Alice hastily
“这对我来说很重要，” 爱丽丝急忙说
"but I'm not looking for eggs, as it happens"
“但我不是在找鸡蛋，就像它碰巧一样”
"and I wouldn't want your eggs anyway"
“反正我也不想要你的鸡蛋”
"I don't like my eggs raw"
“我不喜欢生的鸡蛋”
"Well, be off then!" said the pigeon in a sulky tone
“好吧，那就走吧！” 鸽子用闷闷不乐的语气说
and the pigeon settled down again into its nest
鸽子又回到了它的巢里
Alice crouched down among the trees as well as she could
爱丽丝尽可能地蹲在树林中
her neck kept getting entangled among the branches
她的脖子一直缠在树枝之间
every now and then she had to stop and untwist her neck
她时不时地不得不停下来，解开她的脖子
After awhile she remembered the mushroom
过了一会儿，她想起了那个蘑菇
she still held the pieces of mushroom in her hands
她手里还拿着蘑菇片
and she set to work very carefully
她开始非常小心地工作
first she nibbled at one piece
首先，她啃了一块
and then she nibbled at the other piece
然后她啃了另一块
sometimes she grew taller

有时她会长高
and sometimes she grew shorter
有时她会变矮
but finally she achieved her usual height
但最后她还是达到了平常的高度
she hadn't been her own height for some time
她已经有一段时间没有达到自己的身高了
so everything felt strange for a while
所以有一段时间一切都感觉很奇怪
"The next thing to do is to get into that beautiful garden"
"接下来要做的是进入那个美丽的花园"
"how is that to be done, I wonder?"
"我想知道，这是怎么做到的呢？"
As she said this, she came upon an open place
"说这话的时候，她来到一个空旷的地方
there was a little house, a bit higher than a metre
那里有一座小房子，比一米高一点
"I wonder who lives in this little house"
"我想知道谁住在这栋小房子里"
"I certainly can't go in as big as I am"
"我当然不能像我这样大"
"I would frighten them terribly!"
"我会把他们吓坏的！"
so she nibbled at the little mushroom again
于是她又啃了一口小蘑菇
and soon she brought herself down thirty centimetres
很快，她就把自己降落了三十厘米

A pig and some pepper
一头猪和一些胡椒粉

For a minute or two she stood looking at the house
她站着看了一两分钟，望着房子
suddenly a footman came running out of the woods
突然，一个仆人从树林里跑了出来
he was wearing a special livery uniform
他穿着一件特殊的制服
judging by his face only, she would have called him a fish
仅从他的脸上看，她会称他为鱼
and he rapped loudly at the door with his knuckles
他用指关节大声地敲门
the door was opened by another footman
门是另一个仆人开的
this footman too was wearing a special livery
这个仆人也穿着特殊的制服
this footman had a round face and large eyes like a frog
这个仆人有一张圆圆的脸和像青蛙一样的大眼睛

The footman that looked like a fish initiated the ceremony
看起来像鱼的仆人开始了仪式
he pulled out something from under his arm
他从胳膊下掏出什么东西
and he pulled out from under his arm an envelope
他从胳膊下掏出一个信封
and this envelope he handed over to the other footman
他把这个信封交给了另一个仆人
in a ceremonious tone he told him the orders
他用一种庄重的语气告诉他命令
"This message is for the Duchess"
　“这条信息是给公爵夫人的”
"An invitation from the queen to play croquet"
　“女王邀请你打槌球”
The footman that looked like a frog repeated the order
那个看起来像青蛙的仆人重复了一遍命令
"from the queen"
　“来自女王”
"an invitation"
　“邀请”
"for the Duchess"
　“为了公爵夫人”
"playing croquet"
　“玩槌球”
Then they both bowed low
然后他们俩都低低地鞠了一躬
and the curls in their wigs got entangled together
他们假发上的卷发纠缠在一起
soon the footman that looked like a fish was gone
很快，那个看起来像鱼的仆人就消失了
but the footman that looked like a frog was still there
但那个看起来像青蛙的仆人还在那里
he was sitting on the ground near the door
他坐在门边的地上

he was staring stupidly up into the sky
他愚蠢地盯着天空
Alice went timidly up to the door and knocked
爱丽丝怯怯地走到门前敲了敲门
"There's no use in knocking," said the footman
“敲门也没用，” 仆人说
"and that is for two reasons"
“这有两个原因”
"First, because I'm on the same side of the door as you are"
“首先，因为我和你在同一侧”
"secondly, because they're making so much noise inside"
“其次，因为他们在里面制造了很多噪音”
"no one could possibly hear you"
“没人能听到你”
And there certainly was a most extraordinary noise going on within
而且里面肯定有一种最不寻常的声音
a constant howling and sneezing
不断嚎叫和打喷嚏
and every now and then a sound of great crashing
时不时传来巨大的撞击声
as if a dish or kettle had been broken to pieces
就像一个盘子或水壶被打碎了一样
"How am I to get in?" asked Alice
“我怎么进去呢？”
"Should you get in at all?" said the footman
“你到底应该进去吗？”
"That's the first question, you know"
“这是第一个问题，你知道的”
Alice opened the door and went in
爱丽丝打开门走了进去
The door led right into a large kitchen
门直接通向一个大厨房
the kitchen was full of smoke from one end to the other

厨房从一端到另一端都充满了烟雾
in the middle of the kitchen was the Duchess
厨房中间是公爵夫人
she was sitting on a three-legged stool
她坐在一个三条腿的凳子上
and she was nursing a baby
她正在哺乳一个婴儿
the cook was leaning over the fire
厨师靠在火上
he was stirring a large caldron
他正在搅动一个大锅
and the caldron seemed to be full of soup
锅里似乎装满了汤
"There's certainly too much pepper in that soup!" Alice said to herself
"那汤里肯定有太多的胡椒粉了！" 爱丽丝自言自语道
she said it as best she could without sneezing
她尽可能地说，没有打喷嚏
Even the Duchess sneezed occasionally
就连公爵夫人也偶尔打喷嚏
but the baby's actions were the most noteworthy
但婴儿的行为是最值得注意的
the baby was sneezing and howling alternately
婴儿打喷嚏和嚎叫交替
there was not a moment's pause between howling and sneezing
在嚎叫和打喷嚏之间没有片刻的停顿
There were two creatures in the kitchen that did not sneeze
厨房里有两个生物不打喷嚏
the cook was too busy to sneeze
厨师太忙了，没时间打喷嚏
and the large cat did not seem to mind the pepper
而那只大猫似乎并不介意胡椒

instead, the large cat was grinning from ear to ear
相反，这只大猫却在咧嘴笑得合不拢嘴
"Please would you tell me," said Alice, a little timidly
“请你告诉我，” 爱丽丝有点怯怯地说
"why is your cat grinning like that?"
“你的猫为什么咧嘴笑？”
"It's a Cheshire-Cat," said the Duchess
“这是一只柴郡猫，” 公爵夫人说
"and that's why he's grinning from ear to ear"
“这就是为什么他笑得合不拢嘴”
"I didn't know that a Cheshire-Cat always grinned"
“我不知道柴郡猫总是咧嘴笑”
"in fact, I didn't know that cats could grin," said Alice
“事实上，我不知道猫会咧嘴笑，” 爱丽丝说
"there is much you don't know," said the Duchess
“你不知道的很多事情，” 公爵夫人说
"there is much you don't know and that's a fact"
“有很多你不知道的，这是事实”
Just then the cook took the caldron of soup off the fire
就在这时，厨师把汤锅从火上拿了下来
and at once she started throwing everything within her reach
她立刻开始把所有她能及的东西都扔出去
she threw everything she could at the Duchess and the babe
她把她能做的一切都扔给了公爵夫人和婴儿
first she threw the fire-irons
首先，她扔出了火镣
then she threw a handful of saucepans
然后她扔了一把平底锅
and finally she threw the plates and dishes
最后，她把盘子和盘子扔了出去
The Duchess took no notice of her
公爵夫人没有注意到她
even when she was hit by a plate she did not worry
即使她被盘子砸中，她也不担心

the baby was already howling so much
婴儿已经嚎叫得很厉害了
so it was impossible to say whether the blows hurt the baby or not
因此，无法说这些打击是否伤害了婴儿
"Oh, please mind what you're doing!" cried Alice
"噢，请小心你在做什么！"
and she jumped up and down in an agony of terror
她在恐惧中上蹿下跳
the Duchess offered Alice the baby
公爵夫人为爱丽丝提供了婴儿
"Here! You may nurse the baby a bit, if you like!"
"来！如果你愿意，你可以给婴儿喂奶一会儿！"
and she flung the baby at her as she spoke
"她一边说一边把婴儿扔向她
"I must go and get ready to play croquet with the queen"
"我得去准备和女王打槌球了"
and she hurried out of the room
她匆匆忙忙地走出了房间
Alice caught the baby with some difficulty
爱丽丝好不容易才抓住了婴儿
because it was a very odd-shaped little creature
因为它是一个形状非常奇特的小生物
and the baby held out its arms and legs in all directions
婴儿向四面八方伸出胳膊和腿
"I better take this child away with me," thought Alice
"我最好把这个孩子带走，"爱丽丝想
"they're sure to kill this baby in a day or two"
"他们肯定会在一两天内杀死这个孩子"
"Wouldn't it be murder to leave this baby behind?"
"留下这个孩子不是谋杀吗？"
She said the last words out loud
她大声说出了最后一句话
and the little thing grunted in reply

小家伙咕哝着回答

"you best not turn into a pig, my dear," said Alice

"你最好不要变成一头猪，亲爱的，" 爱丽丝说

"or else I'll have nothing more to do with you"

"不然我就跟你没什么关系了。"

Alice was just beginning to think to herself:

爱丽丝刚刚开始心里想：

"Now, what am I to do with this creature, when I get it home?"

"现在，当我把这个家伙带回家时，我该怎么办？"

but then the little creature grunted a little violently

但随后这个小家伙咕哝了一声

and Alice looked down into its face in some alarm

爱丽丝有些警惕地低头看着它的脸

This time there could be no mistake about it

这一次不会有错

it was neither more nor less than a pig

它既不多也不少于一头猪

so she set the little creature down

于是她把这个小家伙放了下来

and the little creature trot away quietly into the wood

小家伙悄悄地小跑着走进了树林

Alice felt quite relieved to see the creature go

爱丽丝看到这个生物走了，感到相当欣慰

Alice was a little startled by seeing the Cheshire-Cat

爱丽丝看到柴郡猫有点吃惊

it was sitting on a bough of a tree a few yards off

它坐落在几码外的一根树枝上

The cat only grinned when it saw her

猫看到她时只是咧嘴一笑

"Cheshire-cat," began Alice, rather timidly

"柴郡猫，" 爱丽丝颇为怯怯地开始说

"would you please tell me which way I ought to go from here?"

"你能告诉我，我从这里应该走哪条路吗？"

"In that direction," the cat said

"在那个方向，" 猫说

and it waved the right paw around

它挥舞着右爪

"In that direction lives a maker of hats"

"在那个方向上住着一个帽子制造商"

and then the cat waved its other paw

然后猫挥动了它的另一只爪子

"and in that direction lives a march hare"

"在那个方向住着一只三月兔"

"Visit either you like; they're both mad"

"你想去哪儿就去哪儿;他们都疯了"

"But I don't want to go among mad people," Alice remarked

"但我不想和疯子混在一起，" 爱丽丝说

"Oh, you can't help that," said the Cat

"哦，你没办法，" 猫说

"we're all mad here"

"我们在这里都生气了"

"are you playing croquet with the queen today?"

"你今天和女王一起打槌球吗？"

"I would like to very much," said Alice

"我非常想，" 爱丽丝说

"but I haven't been invited yet"

"但我还没有被邀请"

"You'll see me there," said the Cat

"你会在那儿看到我的，" 猫说

and from one moment to the next the cat vanished

从这一刻到下一刻，那只猫消失了

soon Alice got in sight of the house of the march hare

不久，爱丽丝就看到了三月兔的房子

this was a very large house

这是一座非常大的房子

so Alice did not want to go near the house

所以爱丽丝不想靠近房子
first she had to nibble some more of the left side bit of mushroom
首先，她得再啃一些左边的蘑菇

a mad tea-party
疯狂的茶话会

In front of the house there was a tree
房子前面有一棵树
and under the tree there was a table
树下有一张桌子
and the table was set with all sorts of cutlery
桌子上摆满了各种各样的餐具
the march hare and the hat maker were at the table
三月兔和制帽者在桌旁
and together they were having tea
他们一起喝茶
a dormouse was sitting between them
一只睡鼠坐在他们之间
and the dormouse was fast asleep
睡鼠睡着了
The table was of extraordinary size
桌子非常大
but most of the table was unoccupied
但桌子的大部分都没人坐
they sat crowded together at one corner of the table
他们挤在一起坐在桌子的一角
and yet they made excuses when they saw Alice
然而，当他们看到爱丽丝时，他们找了个借口
"No room! No room!" they cried out
"没有房间！没有空间！
"There's plenty of room!" said Alice indignantly
"空间很大！"

at one end of the table there was a large arm-chair
桌子的一端有一把大扶手椅
and Alice sat herself in the armchair
爱丽丝自己坐在扶手椅上
the hat maker opened his eyes very wide
制帽人睁大了眼睛
he couldn't believe what he was seeing
他简直不敢相信自己所看到的
but his mind was curious about other things
但他的头脑对其他事情感到好奇
"Why is a raven like a writing-desk?"
“为什么乌鸦就像写字台？”
Alice was open to the challenge
爱丽丝对挑战持开放态度
"I'm glad they've begun asking riddles"
“我很高兴他们开始问谜语”
"I believe I can guess that," she added aloud
“我相信我能猜到，” 她大声补充道
The march hare grew curious about Alice
三月兔对爱丽丝越来越好奇
"Do you really think you can find the answer?"
“你真的觉得你能找到答案吗？”
"I think I can find the answer indeed," said Alice
“我想我确实能找到答案，” 爱丽丝说
"Then you should say what you mean," the march hare went on
“那你就说出你的意思吧，” 马奇兔继续说
"I do say what I mean," Alice hastily replied
“我说的是我的意思，” 爱丽丝急忙回答
"at the very least I mean what I say"
“至少我说的是真的”
"that's the same thing, you know"
“那是一回事，你知道的”
the dormouse also contributed to the conversation

睡鼠也为这次对话做出了贡献
but the dormouse seemed to be talking in its sleep
但睡鼠似乎在睡梦中说话
"I breathe when I sleep"
  "我睡觉时会呼吸"
"I sleep when I breathe!"
  "我呼吸时睡觉！"
"you might as well say they are the same too"
  "你还不如说他们也是一样的。"
"It is the same thing with you," said the hat maker
  "你也是一样的，" 帽子制造商说
and he poured a little tea on the dormouse's nose
他把一点茶倒在睡鼠的鼻子上
The Dormouse shook its head impatiently
睡鼠不耐烦地摇摇头
and again the dormouse spoke, without opening its eyes
睡鼠又开口了，眼睛没有睁开
"Of course, of course it is the same"
  "当然，当然是一样的"
"that's just what I was going to say myself"
  "这就是我自己要说的"

The hat maker turned to Alice and asked another question
帽子制造商转向爱丽丝，问了另一个问题
"Have you guessed the riddle yet?"
“你猜到谜语了吗？”
"No, I give up," Alice conceded
“不，我放弃了，” 爱丽丝承认
"What's the answer?" she wanted to know
“答案是什么？” 她想知道
"I haven't the slightest idea," said the hat maker
“我一点也不知道，”帽子制造商说
"Nor do I know," said the march hare
“我也不知道，”行军兔说
Alice gave a weary sigh
爱丽丝疲惫地叹了口气
"there are better uses of time than riddles without answers"
“比没有答案的谜语更能利用时间”
"have some more tea," the march hare said to Alice, very earnestly
“再喝点茶吧，” 三月兔非常认真地对爱丽丝说
Alice was quite offended by the offer
爱丽丝对这个提议感到非常不满
"I've had not had tea yet," Alice replied
“我还没喝茶呢，” 爱丽丝回答
"therefore I can't have any more tea"
“所以我不能再喝茶了”
"You mean you can't have less tea," said the hat maker
“你的意思是你不能少喝茶，” 帽子制造商说
"it's very easy to take more than nothing"
“多拿比拿不拿容易”
At this, Alice got up and walked off
“听到这话，爱丽丝起身走了
The dormouse fell asleep instantly
睡鼠瞬间睡着了
and neither of the others took the least notice of her going

其他人都没有注意到她的离开
though she looked back once or twice
虽然她回头看了一两次
they were trying to put the dormouse into the tea-pot
他们想把睡鼠放进茶壶里
"At any rate, I'll never go there again!" said Alice
“无论如何，我再也不会去那里了！”
and she walked her way through the woods
她穿过树林
"that was the stupidest tea-party I've ever been to"
“那是我参加过的最愚蠢的茶话会”
Just as she said this, she noticed something
就在她说这句话的时候，她注意到了什么
one of the trees had a door leading right into it
其中一棵树有一扇门直接通向它
"That's very interesting!" she thought
“那真有趣！”
"I think I may as well go through the door"
“我想我还是进门吧”
And through the door she went
她穿过门走了
Once more she found herself in the long hall
她又一次发现自己在长长的大厅里
again she was close to the little glass table
她又一次靠近了那张小玻璃桌
she took the little golden key
她拿走了那把小金钥匙
and she unlocked the door that led into the garden
她打开了通往花园的门
Then she set to work nibbling at the mushroom
然后她开始啃蘑菇
she had kept a piece of the mushroom in her pocket
她把一块蘑菇放在口袋里
and finally she was about a metre tall

最后，她大约有一米高
then she walked down the little corridor
然后她沿着小走廊走去
and then she finally found herself in the beautiful garden
然后她终于发现自己来到了美丽的花园里
and she was among the bright flower and the cool fountains
她在鲜艳的花朵和凉爽的喷泉之间

The queen's croquet ground
女王的槌球场

A large rose-tree stood near the entrance of the garden
一棵大玫瑰树矗立在花园的入口附近

the roses growing on the tree were white
树上生长的玫瑰是白色的

but there were three gardeners painting the rose
但是有三个园丁在画玫瑰

they were busily painting the roses red
他们正忙着把玫瑰涂成红色

and Alice was watching them paint the roses red
爱丽丝看着他们把玫瑰涂成红色

and suddenly their eyes chanced to fall upon Alice
突然间，他们的目光偶然落在爱丽丝身上

Alice spoke a little timidly
爱丽丝有点怯怯地说道

"Would you tell me, please;"
“请你告诉我吗；”

"why are you all painting those roses?"
“你们为什么要画那些玫瑰？”

five and seven said nothing, but looked at two
五和七什么也没说，只是看着二

two spoke, in a low voice
两个人低声说话

"Why, the fact is, you see, madam"
“哎呀，事实是，你看，夫人”

"this here ought to have been a red rose-tree"
“这儿应该是一棵红玫瑰树”

"and we put a white rose-tree in by mistake"
“我们误把一棵白玫瑰树放进去了”

"as you would agree, the queen must not find out"
“正如你所同意的，女王一定不会发现的”

"else we would all have our heads cut off"
“否则我们都会被砍掉头”

"So you see, madam, we're doing our best"
"所以你看，女士，我们正在尽力而为。"
card five had been anxiously looking across the garden
五号卡一直焦急地望着花园的另一边
At this moment card five called out, "The queen! The queen!"
就在这时，五号牌喊道："皇后！女王！
and the three gardeners instantly scurried away
三个园丁立刻匆匆走开了
and they threw themselves flat upon their faces
他们就倒在地上
There was a sound of many footsteps
传来许多脚步声
Alice looked around, eager to see the queen
爱丽丝环顾四周，渴望见到女王
At the start of the procession were ten soldiers
游行队伍开始时有 10 名士兵
their hands and feet were in the corners
他们的手和脚都在角落里
and in their hands and feet were clubs
他们的手和脚上都有棍棒
next came the ten courtiers
接下来是十个朝臣
the courtiers were ornamented all over with diamonds
朝臣们全身都装饰着钻石
After the courtiers came the royal children
在朝臣之后是皇室子女
there were ten of the royal children
有十个皇室孩子
and all the royal children were ornamented with hearts
所有的皇室孩子都装饰着心形
Next came the guests; mostly kings and queens
接下来是客人；主要是国王和王后
and among the kings and queen Alice saw someone

在国王和王后中，爱丽丝看到了一个人
she saw again the white rabbit she had chased
她又看到了她追赶的那只白兔
The procession was followed the knave of hearts
游行队伍后面是红心之刃
he was carrying the king's crown
他背着国王的王冠
and the king's crown was on a crimson velvet cushion
国王的王冠放在深红色的天鹅绒垫子上
and then came the end of this grand procession
然后，这个盛大的游行结束了
and there at the end were the king and queen of hearts
最后是红心 K 和 Queen
the procession came opposite to Alice
队伍来到爱丽丝的对面
and they all stopped and looked at her
他们都停下来看着她
and the queen said severely, "Who is this?"
王后严厉地问： “这是谁？
She said it to the Knave of Hearts
她对红心之刃说
but he just bowed and smiled in reply
但他只是鞠躬微笑作为回应
Alice spoke very politely
爱丽丝非常有礼貌地说
"My name is Alice, so please your majesty"
“我叫爱丽丝，所以请陛下”
but she had other thoughts to herself
但她心里却有别的想法
"they're only a pack of cards, after all!"
“毕竟，它们只是一包纸牌！”
"Can you play croquet?" shouted the queen
“你会打槌球吗？”
The question was evidently meant for Alice

这个问题显然是针对爱丽丝的

"Yes!" said Alice loudly
　"是的！"

"Come play then!" roared the queen
　"那你来玩吧！"

a timid voice spoke to Alice
一个胆怯的声音对爱丽丝说

"it's a very fine day!"
　"今天真是个晴朗的一天！"

She was walking by the white rabbit
她从那只白兔身边走过

and the White Rabbit was peeping anxiously into her face
白兔焦急地偷看她的脸

"a very fine day indeed," confirmed Alice
　"真是个晴朗的一天，" 爱丽丝肯定道

"Where's the duchess?"
　"公爵夫人在哪儿？"

"Hush! Hush!" said the Rabbit
　"嘘！嘘！

"She's under sentence of execution"
　"她被判处死刑"

"What is she being executed for?" asked Alice
　"她被处决是为了什么？"

"She scuffed the queen's ears," the rabbit began
　"她擦伤了女王的耳朵，" 兔子开始说

the queen shouted in a voice of thunder
女王用雷霆般的声音喊道

"Get to your places!"
　"到你们的地方去！"

and people began running about in all directions
人们开始向四面八方跑来跑去

and they all tumbled up against each other
他们都互相撞了起来

However, they got settled down in a minute or two

然而，他们在一两分钟内就安定下来了
and then the game began
然后游戏开始了
Alice had never seen such a curious croquet ground
爱丽丝从未见过如此奇特的槌球场
the grass was all ridges and furrows
草地上全是山脊和沟壑
The croquet balls were real hedgehogs
槌球是真正的刺猬
and the mallets were real flamingos
木槌是真正的火烈鸟
and the soldiers stood on their hands and feet
士兵们用手和脚站着
because the arches was made from their bodies
因为拱门是由他们的身体制成的
The players all played at once
玩家同时玩
nobody waited for their turns
没有人等待轮到他们
and everyone quarrelled with everyone
大家都和大家争吵起来
and all were fighting for the hedgehogs
所有人都在为刺猬而战
soon the queen was in a furious passion
很快，王后就陷入了愤怒的激情中
and she started stamping about and shouting
她开始跺脚大喊大叫
"Chop off his head!"
“砍掉他的头！”
"Chop off her head!"
“砍掉她的头！”
"Chop all their heads off!"
“把他们的头都砍下来！”
Again Alice thought to herself

爱丽丝又心想

"They're dreadfully fond of beheading people here"
"他们非常喜欢在这里斩首"

"the great wonder is that there's anyone left alive!"
"最神奇的是，竟然还有人还活着！"

She was looking about for some way of escape
她正在寻找某种逃生的办法

she noticed a curious appearance in the air
她注意到空气中出现了一个奇怪的景象

"It's the Cheshire-cat," she said to herself
"是柴郡猫，"她自言自语道

"now I shall have somebody to talk to"
"现在我得找个人谈谈了"

"How are you getting on?" said the cat
"你过得怎么样？"

"I don't think they play at all fairly," Alice said
"我认为他们玩得一点也不公平，"爱丽丝说

and she had a rather complaining tone
她的语气颇为抱怨

"they all quarrel so dreadfully"
"他们都吵得那么可怕"

"one can't hear oneself speak"
"一个人听不到自己说话"

"and they don't seem to play by any rules"
"而且他们似乎不按任何规则行事"

the cat asked Alice a question in a low voice
猫低声问爱丽丝一个问题

"How do you like the queen?"
"你觉得女王怎么样？"

"I don't like her at all," said Alice
"我一点都不喜欢她，"爱丽丝说

Alice thought she might as well go back
爱丽丝觉得她还是回去吧
she wanted to see how the game was going
她想看看游戏进展如何
she went off in search of her hedgehog
她出去寻找她的刺猬
The hedgehog was busy fighting another hedgehog
刺猬正忙着与另一只刺猬战斗
this was an excellent opportunity
这是一个绝佳的机会
she could croquet one hedgehog with the other
她可以用一只刺猬和另一只刺猬槌
but her flamingo was on the other side of the garden
但她的火烈鸟在花园的另一边
the flamingo was rather clumsy
火烈鸟相当笨拙
her flamingo was trying to fly up into a tree
她的火烈鸟正试图飞到一棵树上
She caught the flamingo by the leg

她抓住了火烈鸟的腿
and she tucked the flamingo away under her arm
她把火烈鸟塞到胳膊下
that way the flamingo couldn't escape again
这样火烈鸟就无法再次逃脱
Just then Alice happened to meet the duchess
就在这时，爱丽丝碰巧遇到了公爵夫人
The duchess was now out of prison
公爵夫人现在已经出狱了
She tucked her arm affectionately under Alice's arm
她深情地把胳膊塞进爱丽丝的胳膊下
and then they walked off together
然后他们一起走了
Alice was very glad to find her in such a pleasant temper
爱丽丝发现她脾气这么好，真是太高兴了
She was a little startled, however
然而，她还是有点吃惊
she heard the voice of the duchess close to her ear
她听到了公爵夫人的声音，就在她耳边
"You're thinking about something, my dear"
"你在想什么，亲爱的"
"and that makes you forget to talk"
"这让你忘了说话"
"The game's going on rather better now," Alice said
"比赛现在进行得更好了，" 爱丽丝说
it was one way of keeping the conversation going
这是保持对话进行的一种方式
"it is so indeed," said the duchess
"确实是这样，" 公爵夫人说
"and the moral of that is this:"
"而这其中的寓意是这样的："
"It is love that does it all!"
"是爱成就了一切！"
"Love is what makes the world go around"

"爱是世界运转的动力"

Alice had another explanation

爱丽丝有另一种解释

"it's done by everybody minding his own business!"

"每个人都管自己的事！"

"Ah, well! You could be right"

"啊，好吧！你可能是对的"

"It all means much the same thing," said the Duchess

"这都意味着差不多一样的事情，"公爵夫人说

and she dug her sharp little chin into Alice's shoulder

她把她那尖尖的小下巴挖进爱丽丝的肩膀上

"and the moral of that is this"

"它的寓意是这样的"

"Take care of the sense"

"照顾好感觉"

"and then the sounds will take care of themselves"

"然后声音会自己照顾好"

but then the duchess's arm began to tremble

但随后公爵夫人的手臂开始颤抖

Alice looked up and there stood the queen

爱丽丝抬起头来，女王站在那里

the queen had her arms folded

女王双臂交叉

and she was frowning like a thunderstorm!

她皱着眉头，像暴风雨一样！

"I give you fair warning," shouted the queen

"我给你一个公平的警告，"王后喊道

and she stomped on the ground as she spoke

她一边说着，一边跺着地

"either your head or her head must be off"

"要么你的头，要么她的头必须掉下来"

"Take your choice!"

"随你选！"

"and be quick about it"

"而且要快点"
The duchess made her choice
公爵夫人做出了她的选择
and within a moment the duchess was gone
不一会儿，公爵夫人就走了
Then the queen spoke to Alice
然后，王后对爱丽丝说话
"Let's go on with the game"
"让我们继续游戏"
Alice was too frightened to say a word
爱丽丝吓得一句话也说不出来
and she slowly followed her back to the croquet-ground
她慢慢地跟着她回到了槌球场
the whole time the queen quarrelled with the other players
皇后一直与其他玩家争吵
"Chop off his head!"
"砍掉他的头！"
"Chop off her head!"
"砍掉她的头！"
"Chop all their heads off!"
"把他们的头都砍下来！"
soon all the players were in custody
很快，所有球员都被拘留了
only the king, the queen, and Alice remained
只剩下国王、王后和爱丽丝
Then the queen left, quite out of breath
然后女王气喘吁吁地走了
and she walked away with Alice
她和爱丽丝一起走了
Alice heard the king quietly say something
爱丽丝听到国王悄悄地说了些什么
"You are all pardoned"
"你们都被赦免了"
but suddenly there was another cry heard

但突然又听到了一声哭声
"The trial is beginning!"
"审判开始了！"
and Alice ran along with the others
爱丽丝和其他人一起跑

who stole the tarts?
谁偷了蛋挞？
The king and queen of hearts were seated
红心国王和红心皇后就座
they were on their throne when Alice arrived
当爱丽丝到来时，他们正在他们的宝座上
there was a great crowd assembled around them
他们周围聚集了一大群人
there were all sorts of little birds and beasts
有各种各样的小鸟和野兽
and there was the whole pack of cards
还有整包牌
the knave was standing in front of them, in chains
那把刀站在他们面前，戴着锁链
and there was a soldier on each side to guard him
两边各有个士兵看守他
near the King was the white rabbit
国王身边有一只白兔
he had a trumpet in one hand
他一只手拿着小号
and he had a scroll of parchment in the other hand
他的另一只手里拿着一卷羊皮纸
In the very middle of the court was a table
庭院的正中央有一张桌子
on the table was a large dish of tarts
桌上放着一大盘蛋挞

"I wish they'd get the trial done," Alice thought
"我希望他们能完成审判，" 爱丽丝想
"then we could eat some of those refreshments!"
"那我们就可以吃点东西了！"

The judge, by the way, was the king
顺便说一句，法官是国王
and he wore his crown over his great wig
他把皇冠戴在他的大假发上
"That's the jury-box," thought Alice
"那是陪审团席，" 爱丽丝想
"and those twelve creatures, I suppose they are the jurors"
"还有那十二个生物，我想他们就是陪审员。"

some were animals, and some were birds
有些是动物，有些是鸟
Just then the white rabbit cried out
就在这时，白兔叫了起来
"Silence in the court!"
“法庭上安静！”
"Herald, read the accusation!" said the king
“传令官，读读控告书！”
the white rabbit blew three blasts on the trumpet
白兔吹响了小号三声
then he unrolled the parchment-scroll
然后他展开了羊皮纸卷轴
and he read as follows:
他读到如下：
"The queen of hearts, she made some tarts,"
“红桃皇后，她做了一些馅饼，”
"All this she did on a summer day"
“这一切都是她在一个夏日做的”
"The knave of hearts, he stole those tarts"
“红心之士，他偷走了那些蛋挞”
"And he took those tarts far away!"
“他把那些蛋挞带到了很远的地方！”
"Call the first witness," said the king
“传唤第一个证人，”国王说
and the white rabbit blew three blasts on the trumpet
白兔吹响了号角
"bring the first witness!" he called out
“带来第一个证人！”
The first witness was the hat maker
第一个证人是帽子制造商
he came in with a teacup in one hand
他一手拿着茶杯进来
and he had a piece of bread and butter in the other hand
他的另一只手里拿着一块面包和黄油

"You ought to have finished," said the King
“你应该说完的，” 国王说
"When did you begin?"
“你什么时候开始的？”
The hat maker looked at the march hare
帽子匠看着那只三月兔
the march hare had followed him into the court
三月兔跟着他进了院子
he had walked arm in arm with the dormouse
他和睡鼠手挽手走过
"Fourteenth of March, I think it was," he said
“我想是 3 月 14 日，” 他说
"Give your evidence," said the king
“拿出你的证据，” 国王说
"and don't be nervous, or I'll have you executed on the spot"
“别紧张，不然我会当场处决你。”
This did not seem to encourage the witness at all
这似乎一点也不鼓励证人
he kept shifting from one foot to the other
他不停地从一只脚移动到另一只脚
and he looked uneasily at the queen
他不安地望着王后
and, in his confusion, he bit a large piece out of his teacup
他困惑地从茶杯里咬了一大块
really he meant to bite from his bread and butter
他真的是想咬他的面包和黄油
Just at this moment Alice felt a very curious sensation
就在这时，爱丽丝感到一种非常奇怪的感觉
she was beginning to grow larger again
她又开始长大了
The miserable hat maker dropped his teacup
可怜的制帽匠掉下了他的茶杯
and the bread and butter fell to the ground
面包和黄油掉在地上

and he went down on one knee
他单膝跪地

"I'm a poor man, your majesty," he began
 “我是个穷人，陛下，” 他开始说

"You're a very poor speaker," said the king
 “你是个很差的演讲者，” 国王说

"You may go," said the king
 “你可以走了，” 国王说

and the hat maker hurriedly left the court
帽子制造商匆匆离开了庭院

"Call the next witness!" said the king
 “传唤下一个证人！”

The next witness was the duchess's cook
下一位证人是公爵夫人的厨师

She carried the pepper-box in her hand
她手里拿着胡椒盒

and the people near the door began sneezing all at once
门口附近的人一下子都打了个喷嚏

"Give your evidence," said the king
 “拿出你的证据，” 国王说

"I shall give no evidence," said the cook
 “我不拿任何证据，” 厨师说

The king looked anxiously at the white rabbit
国王焦急地看着那只白兔

and the white rabbit spoke in a quiet voice
白兔小声说道

"your majesty must cross-examine this witness"
 “陛下必须盘问这位证人”

"Well, if I must, I must," the king said
 “嗯，如果我必须的话，我必须，” 国王说

"What are tarts made of?"
 “蛋挞是用什么做的？”

"tarts are made of pepper, mostly," said the cook
 “蛋挞大部分是用胡椒做的，” 厨师说

For some minutes the whole court was in confusion
有几分钟，整个法庭都陷入了混乱
eventually they all settled down again
最终，他们都再次安定下来
but by then the cook had disappeared
但那时厨师已经消失了
"Never mind!" said the king
"没关系！"
"call to the stand the next witness"
"传唤下一位证人出庭"
Alice watched the white rabbit as he fumbled over the list
爱丽丝看着那只白兔摸索着名单
you can imagine her surprise at what she heard next
你可以想象她接下来听到的声音会感到惊讶
at the top of his shrill little voice, he called the name "Alice!"
他用尖锐的小嗓门叫着这个名字"爱丽丝！"

Alice's evidence
Alice 的证据

"Here!" cried Alice
"在这里！"
She jumped up in a great hurry
她急忙跳了起来
and she tipped over the jury-box
她翻倒了陪审团席
and she knocked over all the jurymen
她打翻了所有的陪审团成员
and they fell on to the heads of the crowd below
他们就倒在了下面人群的头上
Alice was in great dismay
爱丽丝非常沮丧
"Oh, I beg your pardon!" she exclaimed
"哦，我求你原谅！"
"The trial cannot proceed," said the king
"审判不能继续，"国王说
"the jurymen must get back in their proper places"
"陪审员必须回到他们应该的位置上"
he repeated the order with great emphasis
他非常强调地重复了这个命令
and he looked at Alice sternly
他严肃地看着爱丽丝
"What do you know about these events?" the king asked Alice
"你对这些事件了解多少？"
"I know nothing on the subject," said Alice
"我对这个问题一无所知，"爱丽丝说
The king then read from his book
然后国王从他的书中读出来
"Rule forty two"
"规则 42"
"All persons more than a mile high are to leave the court"

"所有身高超过一英里的人都要离开法院"
"I'm not a mile high," said Alice
"我没有一英里高，" 爱丽丝说
"Nearly two miles high," said the Queen
"差不多有两英里高，" 王后说

"Well, I refuse to go," said Alice
"嗯，我不肯走，" 爱丽丝说
The king turned pale
国王脸色苍白
and he shut his note-book hastily
他匆匆关上了他的笔记本
"Consider your verdict," he said to the jury
"考虑一下你的裁决，" 他对陪审团说
he spoke in a low, trembling voice
他用低沉、颤抖的声音说
then the white rabbit spoke

然后白兔开口了
"There's more evidence to come yet"
 "还有更多证据"
and he jumped up in a great hurry
他急忙跳了起来
"This paper has just been picked up"
 "这篇论文刚刚被捡起来"
"It seems to be a letter written by the prisoner"
 "这似乎是囚犯写的一封信"
He unfolded the paper as he spoke
他一边说一边展开那张纸
"It isn't a letter, after all"
 "毕竟，这不是一封信"
"what it was was a set of verses"
 "那是一组经文"
"Please, your majesty," said the knave
 "拜托了，陛下，" 小刀说
"I didn't write those verses"
 "那些诗句不是我写的"
"and they can't prove that I wrote anything"
 "他们无法证明我写了什么"
"there's no name signed at the end"
 "最后没有签名"
the king spoke to the knave
国王对 Knave 说话
"You must have meant to cause some mischief"
 "你一定是故意捣蛋的"
"else you'd have signed your name like an honest man"
 "要不然你早就像个老实人一样签上你的名字了"
There was a general clapping of hands
大家都拍手叫好
and the king turned to the white rabbit
国王转向白兔
"Read the verses," he ordered

"读这些经文，" 他命令道

There was dead silence in the court

法庭上一片死寂

and the white rabbit read out the verses

白兔读出诗句

They told me you had been to her

他们告诉我你去过她

And they mentioned me to him

他们向他提到了我

She gave me a good character

她给了我一个好品格

But she said I could not swim

但她说我不会游泳

He sent them word I had not gone

他给他们发了我没有去的消息

We know it to be true

我们知道这是真的

If she should push the matter on, what would become of you?

如果她把这件事推下去，你会怎么样？

I gave her one, they gave him two

我给她一个，他们给他两个

You gave us three or more

您给了我们三个或更多

They all returned from him to you

他们都从他那里回到你身边

although they were mine before

虽然他们以前是我的

If I or she should chance to be

如果我或她有机会

If I or she were involved in this affair

如果我或她参与了这件事

He trusts to you to set them free

他相信你能释放他们

Exactly as we were

和我们一模一样

My notion was that you had been

我的想法是你一直

Before she had this fit

在她有这个

An obstacle that came between

介于两者之间的障碍

Him, and ourselves, and it

他，还有我们自己，还有它

Don't let him know she liked them best

不要让他知道她最喜欢他们

For this must for ever be a secret, kept from all the rest

因为这必须永远是一个秘密，不让其他人知道

This secret must remain a secret between yourself and me

这个秘密必须是你我之间的秘密

the king was very impressed

国王印象深刻

"That's the most important piece of evidence we've heard yet"

“这是我们听到的最重要的证据”

"I don't believe those verses carry an atom of meaning," objected Alice

“我不相信那些诗句有一点意义，” 爱丽丝反对道

the King had his own opinion on the matter

国王对此事有自己的看法

"If there's no meaning in those words, that saves a world of trouble"

“如果这些词没有意义，那就省去了一堆麻烦”

"then we needn't try to find the meaning"

“那我们就不需要试着去找意思了”

"Let the jury consider their verdict"

“让陪审团考虑他们的裁决”

"No, no!" said the queen

"不，不！"

"Sentencing first—verdict afterwards"
"先判刑 后判刑"

"Stuff and nonsense!" said Alice loudly
"胡说八道！" 爱丽丝大声说

"how silly it is to sentence the defendant first!"
"先判刑被告是多么愚蠢啊！"

"Hold your tongue!" said the queen, turning purple
"住嘴！"

"I will not hold my tongue!" said Alice
"我不会闭口不言的！"

the queen shouted at the top of her voice
女王大声喊道

"chop off her head!"
"砍掉她的头！"

Nobody made a movement
没有人动静

"Who cares what you say?" said Alice
“谁在乎你说什么呢？”
she had grown to her full size by this time
这时她已经长到全能的体型
"You're nothing but a pack of cards!"
“你不过是一堆纸牌！”
At this, all the cards rose up in the air
这时，所有的牌都升起了
and all the cards came flying down upon her
所有的牌都飞来飞去
she gave a little scream
她发出了一声小小的尖叫
she was half afraid, but also angry
她半怕半生
and she tried to fight the cards off of herself
她试图从自己身上挣扎
and then she found herself lying on the grass bank
然后她发现自己躺在草地上
her head was in the lap of her sister
她的头靠在她姐姐的腿上
some dead leaves had landed on her face
一些枯叶落在她的脸上
and her sister was gently brushing the leaves away
她的姐姐轻轻地把树叶拂去
"Wake up, Alice dear!" said her sister
“醒醒吧，亲爱的爱丽丝！”
"what a long sleep you've had!"
“你睡得真长啊！”
"Oh, I've had such a curious dream!" said Alice
“噢，我做了个这么奇怪的梦！”
And she told her sister all she could remember
她把她能记得的一切都告诉了她的姐姐
all the strange adventures that you have just been reading about

您刚刚阅读的所有奇怪的冒险

Alice got up and ran off

爱丽丝起身跑开了

and she thought, while she ran, about her dream

她一边跑一边想着她的梦想

"what a wonderful dream it had been!"

“这真是个美妙的梦！”

www.ingramcontent.com/pod-product-compliance
Lightning Source LLC
Chambersburg PA
CBHW011045190726
48290CB00011B/3018

"making a chain of daisies would be a pleasure""制作一串雏菊将是一种乐趣""but is it worth the effort of getting up and picking the daisies??"" 但是，值得起床摘雏菊吗？？"this was not so easy to think about 这可不是那么容易想的 because the day was making her feel sleepy and stupid 因为那一天让她感到困倦和愚蠢 but suddenly her thoughts were interrupted 但突然间，她的思绪被打断了 a White Rabbit with pink eyes ran close by her 一只粉红色眼睛的白兔在她身边跑来跑去

ISBN 978-1-83566-737-8

9 781835 667378